A Beach Day

by Douglas Florian

Greenwillow Books, New York

Black felt pen, crayon, colored pencils,
and watercolor paints were used
for the full-color art.
The text type is Cheltenham.

Library of Congress Cataloging-in-Publication Data

Florian, Douglas.
A beach day / by Douglas Florian.
p.   cm.
Summary: Describes simply how one family enjoys a day at
the beach. Includes a list of seashells for which to look.
ISBN 0-688-09104-0.   ISBN 0-688-09105-9 (lib. bdg.)
[1. Beaches—Fiction.]   I. Title.
PZ7.F6645Be   1990
[E]—dc19
89-1933   CIP   AC

TO BELORIA LALLOUZ

Car ride

Seaside

Parking lot

Find a spot

Feet splash

Waves crash

Kites sail

Sand pail

Shells and stones

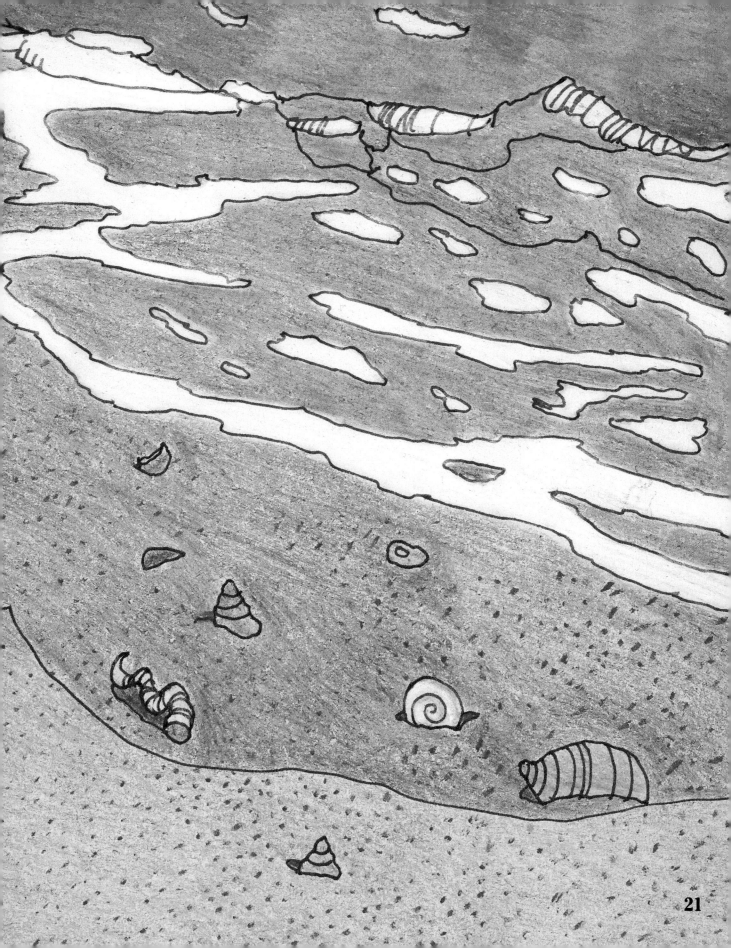

Ice cream cones

Sea gulls squawk

Boardwalk

Sunset sky

Fourth of July!

You can find these shells
on the Atlantic coast and the Pacific coast

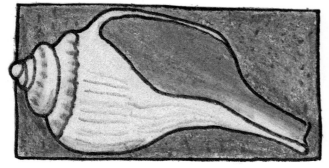

Channeled Whelk

Mud Whelk

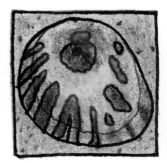

Plate Limpet

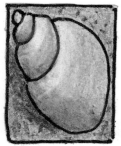

Northern
Chink Shell

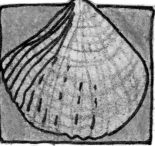

Iceland Cockle

False Angel Wing

Rosy Dove
Shell

Hair Triton

Muller's Nut Clam

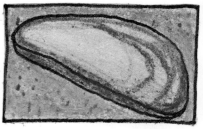

Blue Mussel

Purple Snail

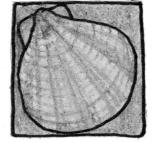

Iceland Scallop

Arctic Natica

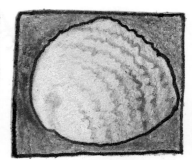

Spiny Slipper Shell